First published in Switzerland under the title *Sara will erzählen*

First published in the United States, Great Britain, Canada,
Australia, and New Zealand in 1995 by North-South Books,
an imprint of Nord-Süd Verlag AG, Gossau Zürich, Switzerland.

Distributed in the United States by North-South Books Inc., New York.

Library of Congress Cataloging-in-Publication Data is available.
A CIP catalogue record for this book is available from The British Library.
ISBN 1-55858-393-9 (trade binding)
ISBN 1-55858-394-7 (library binding)

1 3 5 7 9 TB 10 8 6 4 2
1 3 5 7 9 LB 10 8 6 4 2
Printed in Belgium

Hannelore Voigt

Not Now, Sara!

Illustrated by Olivier Corthésy and Nicolas Fossati

Translated by J. Alison James

North-South Books

New York / London

All the way home from school today, I hugged my new painting. Everyone in my class had done one, and mine had been voted the best! I couldn't wait to show it to my mother. I painted my family: my mother, my father, my little brother Fabian, and my grandma, who lives next door.

When I got home, I stood outside the door and rang the bell. My mother opened the door.

"Oh, it's only you," she said. "Why did you ring the bell?"

I held the painting in my hands. "Because I've got something special to show you," I said.

"Not now, Sara," Mother said. "I'm on the phone."

So I sat down to wait.

When Fabian started to howl, Mother hung up the phone.

"I'm ready," I said.

"Not right now, I have to feed Fabian."

I looked at my little brother. He has such a big mouth. How could such a little kid have a mouth that big? Mother filled it up with food. One spoonful, then another, and another. Disgusting!

"I'm going to Grandma's," I said.

Grandma was all dressed up. She smelled like roses.

"Oh, it's only you, Sara," said Grandma when she let me in. She bent down and gave me a rosy kiss on my cheek. "I was expecting someone else."

I sat down on the sofa, but Grandma didn't sit next to me as usual. The table was set for tea with two cups and plates. Grandma went to the kitchen and brought back a huge cake, with a marzipan rose right in the middle.

"I have something special to show you," I said.

"Not now, Sara. Could you bring it back tomorrow?" Grandma asked. "I'll even save you a piece of cake."

I turned to go, and Grandma walked me to the door. She put her arm on my shoulder. "I haven't seen this fellow for twenty-two years," she said. She gave me a squeeze.

I decided to go to my friend Sophie's house. Sophie had painted a picture of her family too. We could look at each other's pictures and tell funny stories.

Sophie's mother answered the door. She looked busy. "Sophie's not here," she said.

"Where is she?"

"At a friend's house."

"I thought I was her friend."

"Of course you are, Sara. But a person can have more than one friend."

But Sophie is my best friend, I thought as I walked away.

Down the street from Sophie's house was the bank where my father worked. I knew *he* would want to see my painting.

But when I walked into the bank, I saw a row of men behind glass windows, dressed in suits. They looked sad. I didn't even recognize my father until I went right up close.

"Hello, Sara!" he said with a big smile. "Where's Mother?"

"At home," I said.

He looked worried then. "You shouldn't be here alone."

"But I have a painting to show you," I said.

"Not now, Sara. I'll look at your painting when I get home tonight," he said. "You need to go straight home."

But I didn't go home. I kept on walking until I came to the bakery. Nero, the baker's dog, was tied up outside. I often played fetch with Nero when we went to the park in the evenings.

"Hello, Nero," I said.

But Nero growled and barked. He didn't seem to know who I was.

"Who's bothering my dog?" the baker called out of the window.

"It's only me, Sara."

"Nero doesn't like to be disturbed when he's chained up," the baker explained. "You can play with him later when we go to the park."

I passed the building where Mrs. Cohen, my music teacher, lives. Mrs. Cohen was a nice lady. I just knew she'd like to see my painting.

I pushed the buzzer for her apartment.

"Hello?" Mrs. Cohen's voice sounded scratchy over the intercom.

"Hello, it's Sara."

"Sara? But today is Friday."

"I know," I said. "I've just come for a visit."

"Oh, not right now, Sara. I have a student here, and another one is coming in a few minutes."

"Sorry," I said.

"See you Monday!" she said cheerfully.

I kept walking. There were tall buildings all around me filled with people, but nobody wanted to see my picture.

I walked for a long time. I had my whole family tucked under my arm, but I felt lonely.

I found some stairs that led to a park. I was tired and hungry. My feet hurt. I sat down on a bench and took out my picture. There was my father with his big smile. There was my mother, wearing a dress like a queen. There was my grandmother with rosy cheeks. And Fabian even had baby food all over his face.

I loved my family. I missed them. I felt like crying, but instead I lay down on the bench and closed my eyes. I tried to imagine my family. My mother's dress glittered with a thousand sparkles. Fabian stood up, walked to me, and said, "Hello, Sara. Can I see your picture?" My father laughed and said, "Fabian's learned to talk!" Grandma turned to me and said, "Are you all right?"

"Are you all right?"

I sat up, blinking. I was in the park, and an old lady was shaking my shoulder. My family was gone. I was alone and cold.

"Aren't you Irma Rosenblum's granddaughter?"

That was Grandma's name. I nodded.

"You're a long way from home," she said. She sat down next to me. "You look sad. Is something wrong?"

I nodded again. "Nobody will listen to me."

"I'll listen to you. Why don't we talk while I walk you home? It's getting late."

So I walked down the stairs with my grandmother's friend, and told her everything that had happened that day.

When we got to my house, I showed her my painting.

"It really is lovely," she said. "You know what the trouble is?"

"The trouble is that nobody wants to see my painting."

The old woman shook her head. "No, that's not the trouble. It was just the wrong time. All those people would love to see this wonderful painting, but when you asked them, they happened to be busy. Sometimes you have to wait for just the right time."

"But I hate waiting."

The woman laughed and laughed. "I can understand that!"

I opened the door to my house.

"Oh, Sara!" Mother said. "You've been gone a long time. How was Grandma's?"

I didn't answer her. I just stood in the room and felt how warm it was. Fabian's mouth was moving in his sleep. I wondered how long it would be before he could really walk and talk.

"Didn't you have something to show me?" Mother asked.

The warm feeling spread through my whole body. "When do you want to see it?" I asked.

My mother looked at me and smiled.

"Right now," she said.